The Hare and the Tortoise

GW01057586

Contents

The Hare and the Tortoise
A fable by Aesop   2

The Hare and the Tortoise
A fable with a difference   4

Tortoise
A poem   23

From Start to Finish
A map and an email   24

Track Stars Fact Files
Biographical information and a timeline   26

SuperTort and Hairy Hare
A cartoon story   28

Think and Link
Questions to discuss   32

The HARE and the TORTOISE

A fable by Aesop

ONCE there was a very boastful Hare.

At a meeting of all the animals, he said, "I can run faster than anyone else. I challenge any animal to beat me in a race."

The other animals were silent. Except for one. Tortoise said, "I will accept your challenge."

Hare laughed with contempt. "You! Tortoise! The slowest animal of all!"

Tortoise just smiled and said quietly, "Do not boast until you have won the race."

So they agreed on a course and the race began. Hare ran quickly and took the lead. He was so far ahead of Tortoise, and so confident of winning the race, that he lay down to take a nap.

As Hare slept, Tortoise plodded along, step by step. Eventually, Tortoise passed Hare and got closer and closer to the finish line.

Suddenly Hare woke up. When he realised what had happened, he darted to the finish line, but Tortoise crossed it just ahead of him.

"Slow but steady wins the race."

The Hare and the Tortoise

This fable's a change from Aesop's one,
and it tells a story that's even more fun!

Tortoise spent most days eating lettuce leaves by the river bank. When he wasn't eating, he would visit Hare in her beauty salon.

Tortoise was reading the newspaper while Hare gave his shell a good wax and polish.

"Look, Hare," said Tortoise. "There is a fun run tomorrow. There will be lucky prizes at the finish line! I wonder if one of them might be a juicy lettuce?"

"Do you think there will be photographers?" asked Hare. "I would like to have my picture in the paper."

Bright and early the next morning, Hare and Tortoise took their place at the starting line. At the sound of the starter's gun, off they went down the road.

Sitting high on a branch, Owl asked, "Hooooooow will you win the race?"

Tortoise replied, "Slow and steady's the best pace."

Owl hooted, "Good eyesight helps you reach first place."

Hare looked at Owl, then raced back to her salon.

Hare returned wearing some cool sunglasses.

As Tortoise and Hare reached the paddock, Horse asked, "How will you win the race?"

Tortoise replied, "Slow and steady's the best pace."

"Hmph!" neighed Horse. "Strong hoofs and steady feet prevent defeat."

Hare looked at Horse's strong hoofs.
Hare raced back to her salon.

Hare returned wearing some trendy running shoes.

As Tortoise and Hare raced along the lake, Frog asked, "How will you win the race?"

Tortoise replied, "Slow and steady's the best pace."

Frog croaked, "Long thin legs help to give chase."

Hare thought about this. Frog's legs were long, thin and ... shiny! Hare raced back to her salon.

Hare returned wearing some shiny leggings.

At the bottom of the hill, stretched out in the warm sun, Cat asked, "How will you win the race?"

Tortoise replied, "Slow and steady's the best pace."

Cat purred, "Nails that climb will help you reach the finish line."

Back to her salon raced Hare.

Hare returned with long, pointy, painted nails.

Around the bend, beneath the blossoming jacaranda tree, Peacock fanned out his feathers and screeched, "Take great pride in every stride!"

Hare saw all the wonderful colours in Peacock's feathers. And off she raced, back to her salon.

Hare returned wearing an array of brightly coloured ribbons decorating her hair.

Hare and Tortoise could see the finish line, on the other side of the river bank.

Tortoise smiled. "There's not far to go now," he said. "Just across the river."

17

Hare laughed, "Like Owl, I can use my eyes to find the quickest path. Like Horse, I can jump across the water. Like Frog, I can hop from stone to stone. Like Cat, I can creep across the overhanging branch. And like Peacock, I will look beautiful for the photographers."

But Tortoise just lowered his head and plodded along the road. "Slow and steady's the best pace," he muttered to himself.

From log to stone to branch, Hare **hopped, pounced, bounded** and **sprang** into the air.

As Hare slowly surfaced, Tortoise stretched out his long neck over the finish line.

He was very pleased that his shell had been waxed and polished.

Tortoise

hello

tortoise

steady

slow

always   walking

steady, steady,

walking steady, walking slow,

never pausing as you go,

walking ever steady, slow,

steady, never changing pace,

sometimes, tortoise, steady walking,

sometimes slow and steady

walking

wins   the race

From Start to Finish

Find B7 on the map
for the start of the race.
Make your way to the finish,
at your very own pace.

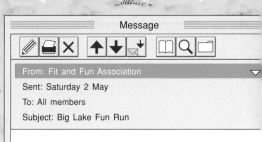

Message

From: Fit and Fun Association
Sent: Saturday 2 May
To: All members
Subject: Big Lake Fun Run

Big Lake Fun Run
8 AM, Saturday 30 May

Take up the challenge! Complete the course in record time, in a personal best time—or just finish! There is NO TIME LIMIT and everyone is a WINNER.

Registration
Register now or register on the day. To download an application form, **click here**.

Start and Finish
The Fun Run starts at map reference B7. It ends at O10. Water will be available at F4 and L2.

Prizes
There will be lucky prizes at the end of the race!

Event Information
For further information on the event, email **info@BigLakeFunRun.com**

TRACK STARS
Fact Files

Here are some stars
who have made big tracks.
You'll be impressed
when you read these facts!

Fanny Blankers-Koen

Date of birth:
26 April 1918

Place of birth:
Lage Vuursche,
Netherlands

Records: World records
in 100 yards, 100 m, 200 m,
high hurdles, high jump,
long jump, pentathlon,
and 4 x 110 yard relay

Olympic medals:
Four gold medals
(100 m, 200 m, 80 m
hurdles and 4 x 100 m
relay), 1948

★ Interesting Fact: Nicknamed "The Fl
Housewife" because she competed in
1948 Olympics when she was 30 year
old and had two children

Modern Olympics Summer Games

1896	1900	1904	1908	1912	1916	1920	1924	1928	1932	1936	1940	1944	1948

No Women
Competitors
　　　　　　　　No Games　　　　　　　　　　　No Games

Glossary

Commonwealth A community of
nations which were once part of
the British Empire.

Marathon A long distance race run
over 42 km. The distance is based
on the legend that in 490 BC, the
soldier Pheidippides (say *fi-dip-i-deez*)
ran 42 km from the town of
Marathon to Athens, to bring the
news of a Greek victory in battle.

Pentathlon An athletic competition
consisting of five events: pistol
shooting, épée fencing, swimming,
riding (equestrian show jumping)
and cross-country running.

Derartu Tulu

Date of birth:
21 March 1972

Place of birth:
Bokoji, Ethiopia

Records: World records
in 10,000 m

Olympic medals:
Two gold medals
(10,000 m), 1992, 2000;
bronze medal (10,000 m),
2004

★ Interesting Fact: Was the first woman
from sub-Saharan Africa to win an
Olympic gold medal

Wilma Rudolph

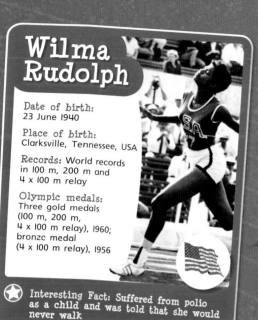

Date of birth:
23 June 1940

Place of birth:
Clarksville, Tennessee, USA

Records: World records
in 100 m, 200 m and
4 x 100 m relay

Olympic medals:
Three gold medals
(100 m, 200 m,
4 x 100 m relay), 1960;
bronze medal
(4 x 100 m relay), 1956

⭐ **Interesting Fact:** Suffered from polio
as a child and was told that she would
never walk

Kelly Holmes

Date of birth:
19 April 1970

Place of birth:
Pembury, Kent,
England

Records: British record
in 1500 m

Olympic medals:
Bronze medal (200 m),
2000; two gold medals
(800 m, 1500 m), 2004

⭐ **Interesting Fact:** Was once the British
Army judo champion

| 1956 | 1960 | 1964 | 1968 | 1972 | 1976 | 1980 | 1984 | 1988 | 1992 | 1996 | 2000 | 2004 | 2008 |

Naoko Takahashi

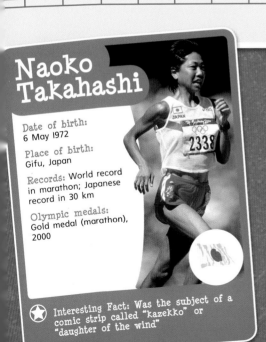

Date of birth:
6 May 1972

Place of birth:
Gifu, Japan

Records: World record
in marathon; Japanese
record in 30 km

Olympic medals:
Gold medal (marathon),
2000

⭐ **Interesting Fact:** Was the subject of a
comic strip called "kazekko" or
"daughter of the wind"

Cathy Freeman

Date of birth:
16 February 1973

Place of birth:
Mackay, Queensland,
Australia

Records: Australian
records in 200 m,
400 m, 4 x 400 m;
Commonwealth
record in 400 m

Olympic medals:
Gold medal (400 m),
2000; silver medal
(400 m), 1996

⭐ **Interesting Fact:** Was the first
Aboriginal athlete to represent Australia
at the Olympics

SUPERTORT and Hairy Hare

Read the story of Supertort, the Hero in a Shell.
This exciting tale has pictures as well.

1

One morning, mild-mannered Torvil Tortoise is relaxing between emergencies.

2

Beep! Beep! A call comes in on the secret TortPhone. Someone is in danger!

3

Torvil becomes the amazingly fit SuperTort! He's ready for adventure.

4

Oh no! It's a raging fire at Mandeville Mansions! Lois Llama may still be inside.

5 But down below, SuperTort spies Hairy Hare lurking in the bushes. What is he doing there?

6 *Help!*

Lois Llama is at an upstairs window crying for help. "Do not fear! I'll save you!" says SuperTort.

7 *My hero!*

SuperTort swoops down and scoops her up in his Super arms. Off they fly to safety.

8 Over a cup of Vita Lettuce and a grass bun, Lois tells SuperTort that she doesn't know how the fire started.

9 SuperTort suspects Hairy Hare. But will our superhero get the evil villain to confess?

10 Leaving Lois in the care of her friends, SuperTort flies back swiftly to Mandeville Mansions.

11 A-ha!

Look! Hairy Hare is there. He is leaving, loaded down with Lois's jewellery.

12 SuperTort lands in front of him. The Hare drops his loot. He grovels on the ground in front of SuperTort.

"You snivelling coward," cries SuperTort. "Admit your guilt!"

"It was me, it was me!" sobs Hare. "Don't hit me!"

Strong SuperTort flies the subdued Hairy Hare to a well-deserved spell in jail.

"We, the people of the town, thank you and wish you well. Cheers to you, brave SuperTort, our Hero in a Shell."

"Hare today and gone tomorrow," smiles SuperTort.

Think and Link

Fables

How are the two versions of the fable the same? How are they different?

Which version of the fable did you like most? Why?

Sequence of Events

Choose two texts. How do they present a sequence of events? What words or symbols are used to mark the sequences? In what other ways could events have been shown in sequence?

Map and Fable

How are the race courses on the map and in the second fable similar? How are they different?

Rhyme, Rhythm and Repetition

In which texts do you find rhyme, rhythm and repetition? What do these features add to these texts?

Map and Email

Why do you need the map when you read the email?

Tortoise Pictures

Which of the tortoise illustrations in this book are most realistic? Which are least realistic? Why?

Which pictures show a view from above? Why has the illustrator chosen this perspective?

Biographies and Cartoon Story

How do these texts describe "heroes"? What personal qualities does a hero have?

What other texts in this book describe heroes? What qualities do these heroes have?